BROOM, ZOOM!

For Billie Cohen Allee
—C. L. C.

For Primo.
And for Viola, as always
—S. R.

SIMON & SCHUSTER BOOKS FOR YOUNG READERS • An imprint of Simon & Schuster Children's Publishing Division • 1230 Avenue of the Americas, New York, New York 10020 • Text copyright © 2010 by Caron Lee Cohen • Illustrations copyright © 2010 by Sergio Ruzzier • All rights reserved, including the right of reproduction in whole or in part in any form. • SIMON & SCHUSTER BOOKS FOR YOUNG READERS is a trademark of Simon & Schuster, Inc. • For information about special discounts for bulk purchases, please contact Simon & Schuster Special Sales at 1-866-506-1949 or business@simonandschuster.com. The Simon & Schuster Speakers Bureau can bring authors to your live event. For more information or to book an event, contact the Simon & Schuster Speakers Bureau at 1-866-248-3049 or visit our website at www.simonspeakers.com. • Book design by Laurent Linn • The text for this book is set in Litterbox ICG. • The illustrations for this book are rendered digitally. • Manufactured in the United States of America • 1010 PCR • 10 9 8 7 6 5 4 3 2 • Library of Congress Cataloging-in-Publication Data • Cohen, Caron Lee. • Broom, zoom! / Caron Lee Cohen ; illustrated by Sergio Ruzzier.—1st ed. • p. cm. • Summary: One beautiful, starry night, a little witch wants to go for a ride on a broom but first she must help a little monster clean up a mess. • ISBN 978-1-4169-9113-7 (hardcover) • [1. Brooms and brushes—Fiction. 2. Cooperativeness—Fiction. 3. Witches—Fiction. 4. Monsters—Fiction.] I. Ruzzier, Sergio, ill. II. • Title. • PZ7.C65974Bs 2010 [E]—dc22 2009000581

BROOM, ZOOM!

Caron Lee Cohen

Illustrated by Sergio Ruzzier

SIMON & SCHUSTER BOOKS FOR YOUNG READERS
New York   London   Toronto   Sydney

"I want the broom."

"I need it now."

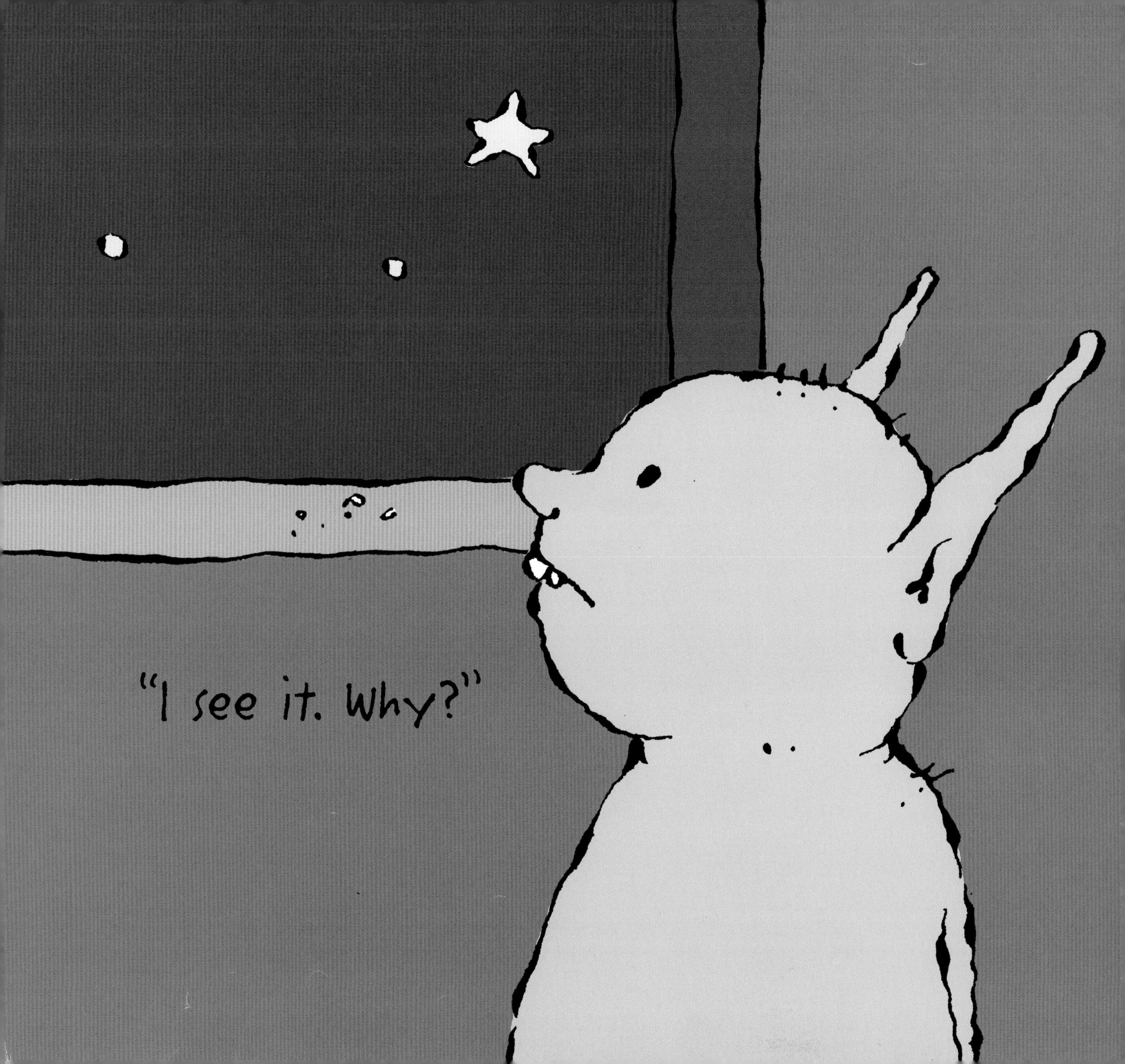

"I see it. Why?"

"To fly it. Want to fly?"

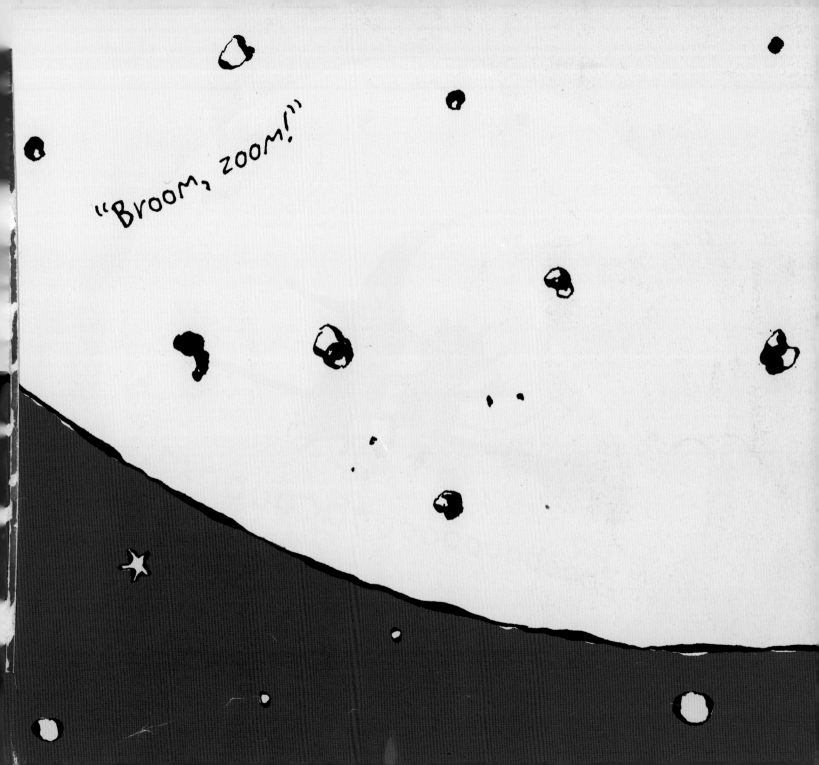